Peppa Pig

and the

Busy Day at School

First paperback edition 2014

Library of Congress Catalog Card Number 2012947254
ISBN 978-0-7636-6525-8 (hardcover)
ISBN 978-0-7636-7227-0 (paperback)

15 16 17 18 19 APS 10 9 8 7 6 5

Printed in Humen, Dongguan, China

This book was typeset in Peppa.
The illustrations were created digitally.

Candlewick Entertainment
An imprint of Candlewick Press
99 Dover Street
Somerville, Massachusetts 02144

visit us at www.candlewick.com

Peppa Pig

and the
Busy Day at School

CANDLEWICK
ENTERTAINMENT

It's Special Talent Day at school,

and Peppa is very excited. She has many different talents, so she hasn't decided which one to share.

"Maybe I will jump rope," says Peppa.

"Or sing or dance."

Mummy Pig, Daddy Pig, Peppa, and George eat a good pancake breakfast.
Then they get in the car
and go to school.

Peppa's friends have already arrived.
Pedro Pony, Candy Cat, and
Rebecca Rabbit are there.

"Good morning,"

says Madame Gazelle.
"Are you ready for Special Talent Day?
We'll share our talents
this afternoon. But first we
have a busy day."

The class
practices counting.

"One, two, three,
four, five,"
begins Madame Gazelle.

"SIX, SEVEN,
EIGHT,
NINE, TEN!"

shouts the class.

Then Madame Gazelle asks the class to name things that begin with each letter of the alphabet.

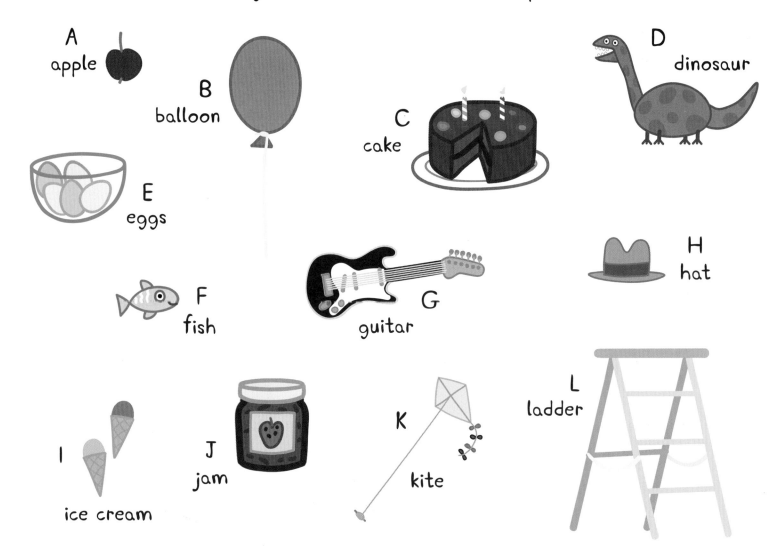

A apple

B balloon

C cake

D dinosaur

E eggs

F fish

G guitar

H hat

I ice cream

J jam

K kite

L ladder

M monkey

N newspaper

O owl

P pizza

Q queen

R rocket

S scooter

T truck

U umbrella

V violin

W watermelon

X xylophone

Y yarn

Z Zoe Zebra!

Then it's time to play store.
Peppa and Suzy are the shopkeepers.

"What would you like?" asks Peppa.

"Do you have any cookies?" asks Danny Dog.

"No," says Peppa, "but we do have a toy telephone. That will be one dollar."

"Thank you," says Danny Dog.

"Do you have a loaf of bread?"
asks Pedro Pony.
"No," says Peppa,
"but we do have a dollhouse!"
"Well, okay," says Pedro.

"What can I buy for a hundred dollars?"
asks Rebecca Rabbit.
"How about a carrot?" says Peppa.
Everyone laughs.

Next it's time to paint.
Peppa wants to teach George how to paint a flower.

"Make a circle," says Peppa.

George paints a green circle.
Then he paints a green zigzag line.

"That's not right, George," says Peppa.
George keeps painting.

Madame Gazelle looks
at Peppa's painting.
"What a lovely flower,"
she says.

"And George has
painted a dinosaur.
Perfect!"

At lunchtime, Peppa and George eat sandwiches with Danny Dog. There's watermelon for dessert!

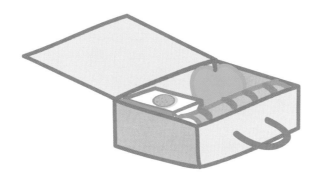

Hooray!

Recess!

Everyone heads outside to the playground.

There's a new tire swing and Peppa wants to try it. She squeezes in.

"Help!" she cries. "I'm stuck!"

Peppa looks funny in the swing.

But Peppa doesn't think being stuck is funny. Her friends try to help.

They pull and pull and pull. Pop! Out comes Peppa!

"Let's play on the slide," she says.

"It's time for **music, music, music!**" sings Madame Gazelle. "Everyone choose an instrument."

Danny chooses the bongo drums.

"Look, I've got cymbals," says Rebecca.

Zoe gets maracas, Freddy chooses a triangle, and Pedro has a tambourine.

Everyone plays together: Boom, bang, crash!

"Oh, my!" cries Madame Gazelle.
"That sounds a bit more like noise than music!"

"Let's go one at a time... then each of you can join in."

Ting, ting, ting
goes the triangle.

Boom, boom, boom
goes Peppa's bass drum.

Bang, bang, bang
go the bongo drums.

Crash, crash, crash, go the cymbals.

Shake-a, shake-a, shake-a go the maracas.

"Lovely!" says Madame Gazelle.

Finally, it is time for Special Talents.
Everyone takes a turn.

Danny Dog's special talent is drumming.

Bang, bang, bang.

Pedro Pony does a magic trick.
Everyone closes their eyes, and
he makes a glass of water disappear.

Zoe Zebra sings.

Candy Cat jumps rope.

Oh, no, thinks Peppa. Now I can't do either of those.
It's a good thing I'm good at dancing, too!
Then Suzy Sheep gets up. "I'm going to dance," she says.

"Oh, no," says Peppa.

"What's the matter?" asks Madame Gazelle.

"I don't have a special talent
that hasn't been done already,"
says Peppa.

"Of course you do," says Madame Gazelle.
"Think of something you really like to do."

Peppa is quiet. She thinks. Then she smiles.
"I know!" she says. She grabs her boots. "Follow me!"

"I'm the best at jumping in muddy puddles!"

Peppa jumps
in a muddy puddle.

Then everyone jumps
in muddy puddles!

"This has been a very good day at school," says Peppa.

And it has.